<u>Index</u>

- Blackened Skies
- Asunder
- Watching you, judging you
- Death
- Fillet Knife
- Forgive me
- Helpless in knowing
- Higher
- Love
- Marked with murder
- Natures rage
- A friend of death
- The House of Dark
- A Russian Plot
- We prepare for war
- Unworthy
- My Weapon, My pen

Fore Word

Not many read the fore word, not many read at all.
A simple few sentences, a dedication, a tribute, to the Lord.
Words of pain and sight, of nightmares that are a real life.
Without the Lord, I would be the nightmares that creep into your dreams, I would be the reason for your screams.

Before you lay your head down to sleep, pray for salvation, for forgiveness.

Eyes in the skies

Stretched, pulled,
Yanked, dislocated shoulders,
Weighted with the world's sorrows.

Middle, middle, torn apart by them all,
Fight, resist, desist, persist,
Shells clinking on concrete roads crumbling,
Dust choking lungs that don't want to breathe anymore of this.

I told you, I told you,
I could say it so!

Let them stretch me, pull me, contort me,
Let them tear me to pieces,
Let them savagely destroy me,
I can't care for them all,
I cannot defend or approve this world,
From my eyes and heart to your mind that knows.

I do not defend or approve this world.
tell them who truly rules them all.

© DM Watterson
21.10.2019

Drawn

You are drawing me,
Or am I drawing you?

Why do I hear you like you are by my side,
Like you are climbing in and out of my mind.
I can hear you clear as a bell,
I can hear your laughter rumble through your belly, through me, as If I am laughing as
well.

I can feel you,
Your breath on my neck,
Your touch when I am peaceful,
Your warmth against my back and legs.

I have nothing valuable to give,
Just a broken heart,
Just a broken soul,
Just a torn and dirty sheet with a few drawings on,
Marked with pieces of coal;
drawn a long time ago.

Drawn to you, drawn to you as home.

© DM Watterson
15.07.2019

Inside of me;

How did I get here?
Why am I inside,
What is this place?
This place of electric wires hanging dead,
This place of court rooms,
This place of solid wood.
Broken features, broken fixtures,
And big glass windows?

A garden outside, full of graves,
Surrounded by dogs old and grey,
All looking down into the coffin lowering, to where it stays.

I walk into a bedroom from my childhood;
My mother and dead father asleep in it,
Yanking on the curtains, trying to let in the light,
all blinded and deaf from the night.

Mercenaries? How did mercenaries get inside?
Standing in each corner of a stone cell,
Rifles, AK-47's, and ammunition rounds held shoulder high.

Down a runway, I see myself dressed in a long flowing gown,
I am holding the hand of the man said to be the love of my life,
Just up a head on the red carpet,
A man waiting in a lobby,
At the bottom of a set of stairs.

I look the other way,
I see me as a kid, no older than 11 years of age,
Shouting at the spirits around me;
"This way!
Find the light, I will lead you to the true Magus!"

Into another room;
There I am, on my knees,
Surrounding by these guns and mercenaries,
A prisoner, captive and held,
Dirty hands, dirty face,

Tortured, in pain,
holding and throwing bones on stone floors,
my hands bleeding,
How can I see myself in the third person?!

How did I get inside my own soul?

I start screaming, wishing I was dreaming,
But I am inside, inside here, somewhere,
Deep within, clawing my way out,
Inch by inch.

© DM Watterson
23.10.2019

Awake

Restless legs,
Spine contorting,
Stretching, arching.
Let me sleep, won't you?

Fingertips touching my skin,
Grazing up and down,
Snagging my skin,
Roughly callused hands touching me with practiced sublime.

Why, and when,
A little girl, and a man,
Now and then,
Thirty years later, the hunt begins again.

I know you; I knew you then,
I know you know,
I am yours; so, you say,
you are mine, say your eyes.

You touch me and I melt and sigh,
Your warm arms are where I die.
Your mouth on mine,
Your sword piercing my mind,
As you shield me with your wings and haphazard smile.

One move, and deep I go on the path of bliss,
A dark and urgent awakening is beginning again,
Pulling me seductively to my death,
Rumpled sheets tangling us together in this bed.

Awake;
Aware, Alive.
Bringing back from the dead this life,
Wrapped in arms and legs and in-between thighs,
Clawing down backs leaving red lines of fire.

Bold, and Bolder.

Flickering history before eyes,
Revolutions, swords, shields, wars and fires,
Broken stairwell leading to the height of all life,
Escalating, escalated, accelerated by the blind;
The end, the end of mankind.

Precipice of consequence,
A cross road upon the edge of being,
Overlooking the devil plague coming for humanity;
Disguised as liberty, disguised as a missionary,
Hiding behind lies of eon old visionaries.

Contemplation of integration,
A momentous movement of hesitation;
"what lies beneath the lies?"
How many deceptions can one being find, and
how many eyes have cried tears dry?

Bold, and bolder,
Smoke and ghosts of voices chosen,
What is his holiness,
When silenced by the noisiness of fallen souls held in chained sentences?

© Delia M Watterson
16.04.2019

:

Ditty

I saw you again today;
But, about an hour and a half before;
I was asked if I had seen you before,
by a lady that watched you,
piss up against a wall.

I looked at her nervously and said;
Yes,
I did,
Once;
but not anymore.
I said you had grown much more than more.

In my mind I saw the cogs and wheels in hers going around and round.
I sadly and secretly told her;
who you really were in my life.

She stood horrified as I explained my heartache over a death,
Your words repeatedly said;
"go wash" three times a long deep knife in my chest.
When you kicked me to the curb,
and that very wet night;
that I decided to leave because I didn't want to fight.

She laughed and said;
Sounds like a little boy still attached to mommy's skirt.

I smiled and laughed as I felt the little hurt in my heart;
Less than the chest pains I have felt since our parting.

I was going to feel pity;
But then I remembered all the things you did that were shitty;
And I decided to instead;
write this rhyming little ditty,
As Ditty rhymes with….
And as long as I am here, or you are alive,
you will always be trying to punish me;
for my life.

© DM Watterson
17.07.2019

Fucking Me & Fucking You

Blood boiling at a temperature unmeasured,
Rage clouding just about every sense to censored.
Bent over without the chance to even get wet;
Unless you count your blood and the tears you have wept.

Fucking you, in every single department.
REVENUE, GRANTS, OPORTUNITY, PERSPERATION, & GOVERNMENT!

Fucking you, fucking me, every chance they get.
EVEN THOUGH WE NEVER ASKED FOR IT!

Fucking you, like you enjoy it.
Fucking me, like I looked for it.

Fucking me, fucking you,
Fucking all of us,
Fucking us blind from the known truth,
Fucking us all until we leave or move.

#Politics

© **D. M Watterson**
12.06.2019

Keep it.

Keep your lies,
Keep your promises,
Keep it all,
On me don't vomit it.

Sinking swiftly, deeply,
Falling, falling,
Closer to the impact of it all burning.

Keep it, steal for it, creep for it, lie and be deceitful for it,
I wouldn't want it anymore.
Take your games,
Take you bullshit list of names,
Take it fucking all!

You pisssed off the god's of war,
You called death to come,
You called pestilence as an old friend,
And famine;
you sleep with every night in your bed!

Keep it.

© DM Watterson
21.10.2019

Love at War;

a dammed tragedy;
or a string of multiplicities?
A yoke of life, of loves and hearts broken over time?
A line drawn, broken, moved and redrawn with its blurry lines?

Evil stands and smiles down upon my bowed head;
As I pray with desperation,
Until my words sound like humming breath.

I call upon the divine, all the angels, and all its guides;
Help me to help them, please, they don't see what is coming, they don't see what is
happening.

My blood drips from my open palms;
As they mistake my pagan sacrifice of my blood with acts of God.
I look down and feel evil mocking me,
Its heat and hatred warming the air I breathe.

Flushing my face, it's so close;
Touching my skin,
My neck,
My shoulders.

I call upon the divine, all the angels, and all its guides;
Help me to help them, please, they don't see what is coming, they don't see what is
happening.

Love at War;
No peace seen;
No life, no wonder, nothing will be.

© DM Watterson
20.06.2019

None

I sit and sigh,
As the arrows and swords gather in the skies;
Beacons of lies held up by the highest.
I sit and try not to cry;
As I see flashes from my minds eye come to life.
Dancing and reshaping like a kaleidoscope held up to the light.

Red flags, and red script;
Like the ink is blood dripped.
Held up signs in the street;
images of stark hatred for your eyes to meet.

I sit and start to scribe;
As the tears well up in my eyes.
My chest closes with the pain of running out of time;
And my ears ring with the sound of my blood pumping throughout.

Scrawling's to explain the seen;
Verses of truth gleamed within them,
Hunted down through cookies and algorithms.

None are safe;
None are free,
None live,
None be.

© DM Watterson
01.10.2019

Not You, Never You;

Just like her, you are too.
Help?
Not her, Never her,
And;
Not you, Never you.

Selfish, vain, an egomaniac,
Just like her, you are too.
Help?
Not her, Never her,
And;
Not you, Never you.

Cold, calculating, spiteful and malicious,
Just like her, you are too.
Help?
Not her, Never her,
And;
Not you, Never you.

Your opposition,
Anyone seeking it,
Any innocent,
But;
Just like her, you are too.
Help?
Not her, Never her,
And;
Not you, Never you.

© D M Watterson
31.07.2019

War

Deadly red beacons seen across the sky;
A peaceful blue soul trying to hold back earths demise.
Shooting like rockets, fierce and faster than light.
A speed that blurs before your eyes.
Unstoppable;
A force that can destroy all of mankind,
With its thirst for Uranium and its determination to survive.

© **DM Watterson**
08.06.2019
#NuclearWar

Riddle #9 - Crowns fall down

Have you ever met a man that plays the game?
Not a player, but a strategist in war games?
A giver and a taker in the same breath?
A liar claiming truths, to disguise his true evilness.
An Admission of "truth", to dissuade the world from the truth of the lies breathed,
With ease; with every breath.

Evil lies behind cold and pretending innocent eyes; trying to lull the world into a slumber
of trust and promise, but truly a marker and player in the game of demise.
You know him as ……… Duress, duress, not a damsel, but a man in a dress.

Rhymes with ….Duress, Distress, but abbreviated to 3 consonants- it rhymes the best.

© D M Watterson
30.09.2019

Without, within:

To the town of sin,
To the land of Ismael,
Where it all began and begins....

Within, within, within;
In sin,
Captive,
In,
Captive,
With,
Captive,
is.

A slave, a runaway,
birthed a noble,
Running, hiding,
As the guards watch with lustful eyes each day deciding.

As prophesized,
A highness;
A Crown with shining eyes.

"Unleash the raptures,
The vultures,
The carrions, and the crows,
To pull and strip this flesh from my bones!"

Within, within, within!

Wings of an Angel;
Spreading, bleeding,
Ripped, torn,
Healing...

Before the last war begins.

© DM Watterson
22.10.2019

Woe of the foe

Woe of the foe,
That follows and seeks,
Woe of the foe,
Who smiles and greets,
Woe of the foe,
Whose paths shall meet,
Woe of the foe,
In-between clandestine sheets,
Woe of the foe,
The temple and the bullet seen,
Woe of the foe.

Woe of the foe;
this woeful Wednesday defeats.

16.10.2019

Woman

She will love you at your darkest,
And tease you at your lightest,
She will hold you when you are alone,
So tight,
because she knows,
and she feels like home.
She will wipe your tears that you hide,
While smiling lovingly into your eyes.

She will treat you like her only,
Like you and her are destined and fated to be,
The most understanding, the most patient,
She will be the warmest, the kindest you ever met,

Don't anger her,
Don't lie to her,
Don't make her sad,
Don't be cruel, and especially don't be glad about it.

She will walk away from you when angry,
You know her cruelty when she no longer feels for you,
She no longer cries for you,
She no longer tries for you,
she leaves you to find your own way,
and worse;
She will treat you as you treated her,
She will speak to you like you speak to her,
She will mirror every evil deed you do and did,
She is truly wicked,

A Woman,
who will make you wish;
That you never did what you did,

© D M Watterson
06.08.2019

Wisdom of a new dawn

Eclipses block out the skies;
When wisdom and folly start to fight,
When missiles concealed, launch in the final hours of life.
Storm clouds gather and block out the sun,
When life is assembled in a line of death, and the fire has been stoked enough already.
Pain pelts down upon those without and refusing refuge,
While winds blow debris into knowledge now compromised with truth.

Waves crash upon the shores of consciousness,
As life and death exchange handshakes and kisses,
Both masks bare in all their beauty and ugliness.
Trees uproot and wander to deeper soils,
While life decays and pest's takeover the spoils.
Life and death are friends and equals,
They balance the scales without outside effort.

Soils subsiding, eroding and dying,
As the "knowledgeable" test the waters of trying.
Wisdom of war, before the death of all,
As the child of the fall is already born,
And will not bathe in blood, but in the wisdom of a new dawn.

© DM Watterson
23.07.2019

Tug of war;

I pull one way, you the other,
I want you, you want me, to be in and out of each other.
Yet here we are playing Tug of war;
I pull one way, you the other,
I want you, you want me, to be in and out of each other.
Yet here we are playing Tug of War instead of being lovers.

© D M Watterson
30.05.2019

Tick Tock your feet

If hell was a stage,
And earth was a witch,
dressed in red and black fishnet,
with boots thigh high.

Make your instrument sing,
make it croon,
and let it reach ears-

waiting for a heavenly hymn!

As emotions turn robotic and dance out in practiced stance.

Nodding, sighing, gasping, and clutching at broken and fallen hearts.

Counting out metronome ticks and tempo beats,
That tick and tick, and tick to tick, to tick, to tock your feet.

A rocking motion to the left,
A sway of hips to the right,
....
And a drum roll,
at the right time.

Tick tock your feet.

The rarity – Mr. Scared of Me

The rarity or the scarcity,
Well not anything willy,
And you will class it as silly:
But every now and then...... it pops....
in real life;

like an Amityville horror scene,
or a house fit for haunting,
or a blocked artery slowly choking the life from you.

No cute doll,
No rosy cheeks.

Queen of the dammed nothingness,
Hunting you, hunting you!

Dominating you like a bitch!

I see you rarity,
Mr. scared of me,
Mrs. I can do whatever I feel.

Do you see me too?
Watching me, watching you,
Eyes in the skies via satellite,
Watched and tolled by a mobile phone every night;
You are not the only eyes that spy;
Go home and cry- how your way turned out.

Mr. Scared of Me,
You are so very entertaining,
Mr. Scared of me, little old me, this old thing,
Terrifying,
Death defying,
Magic linings climbing ceiling of dreams and beliefs'
in a freedom breathed.... that you can never feel.

Oh whist, our way has lost its day,
As time Mr. Scared of me,
It has run away,
Just as with every ending,
Come the truth,

The finger of death is pointing at you.

{The little girl that is/and the woman inside- HUMAN IS WHAT WE ARE- it comes from our heart.}

I could play it,
The tears that have been hidden,
The tears that have been cried,
The dreams buried deep,
The screaming, constant in a mind.
The woman trapped, tied up and bound.

I could play it,
The chords from a heart,
The chords playing from the start,
The song that drowns out the screaming,
The song that numbs the bleeding,
Our blood dripping down chained wings freely.

I could play it,
The words we learnt together,
The words etched and imparted,
The song the heart is made to sing,
The song we wrote together, you and me.
The song that we saw one day would be.

I could play it,
Our song, the one we wrote,
For humanity to wake and see.
The song we wrote in pain and suffering,
The song more beautiful than beauty is,
More than our yearning, a whole lifetime of it.

The lady and her daughter

Pulling her hand;
"come on mommy, come on!
We have to go now!
Come on!"

She stands looking sad,
Hesitant to move,
Again, I grab her hand.

"Mommy Please!
Mommy we have to leave!
They are coming!
Mommy they are going to kill us, please!"

She stands not wanting to move at all,
No will, no life,
Yet alive.

"Mommy please!"
Tears streaming down my cheeks,
I can hear them coming,
Smashing the door down to get in.

Now I am just screaming;
"MOMMMEEEEEEE!
MOMMMEEEEE!
MOMMMMEEEEE!"

As they drag her away from me,
They hold me back separately,
And to the temple they lead me.

Just to wake in this world,
Sweating,
And hard breathing;
Clothes clinging to me wetly,
I hold back the tears in my eyes threatening.

© DM Watterson
28.08.2019

Such Sorrow

Such sorrow,
Sobs held back by a heart conscious of eyes upon it,
Because it has started.
A day that has been dreaded since childhood,
A day that has haunted and plagued since memory could fathom its own grace and name.
A day that shall be marked in blood red stains,
As the beast in the east, and the west;
start the war games.

Such sorrow,
As the gate stands and watches the gone tomorrow,
The scorched earth,
The broken and crumbling cities falling,
Before the new day has come to its dawning.
A day seen by all the world,
A day on the precipice of the greatest war.

Such sorrow as the gate stands silent in-between death and war,
In between the pillars to the temple of benevolence and judgement,
as they start to crumble and fall.
Such sorrow as the dead rise to greet the dying yet to join them,
Such sorrow as the living will never be the same again, despite warning.

© DM Watterson
17.05.2019

See I, See I, See I.

I see, I see, I see;
said the caterpillar to me,
I see I see I see!

Look at my cocoon, how big it's got;
I am going to be the prettiest butterfly the world has ever spotted!

My wings will spread,
Colored with blue, black, silver, and magenta dust,
With streaks of red, and orange and razer barbs to stop others from catching me for luck.

I see, I see, I see.

Swooping down,
without hesitation;
A predator spots the Caterpillar in a state of hibernation;
Before it can cocoon itself,
crushed in bills and claws,
before it could say "I see";
once more.

© DM Watterson
22.07.2019

Plastic man

Who are you plastic man?
You are not the devil surely,
But once I have seen you come out of me ferociously.

Plastic man are you from Space?
When you touch me,
I can't move, your touch causes paralysis.

I was walking in a cellar
When we first met,
I was fine, I was about three,
In my skirt and purple shirt dressed.

Then I saw people wanting to hurt me,
soldiers running after me,
So, I turned to leave,
But then I grew bigger,
And you came out of me?

Plastic man, are you ugly,
You are different, yes,
ugly and obscene.

Why do you visit so infrequently?
Just like the lady.
Why are you both watching over me?
What did I do so wrong?
Why do I need watching over constantly when I never harm anybody?

How are you able to climb in and out of my soul with such ease?

Do you want it?
My dreadlocks and colorful jocular soul of woe?
It doesn't at all seem to be valuable to anyone I know.
Do you want it?
The prisms of light and crystals that weight me down?
That give light to the shadows that follow me from Earth to the beyond.

You can't have it, even if you want it,
My Soul, it is important to you to have it, I will continue to walk with the dead-on earth.
All I ask is you leave me alone,
scared to have no beyond to go to,

that I will never find all I have ever wanted;
a family, love, and my home.

Mother Earth

I hear your cries;
From the pain inflicted by mankind,
Your tears are flowing, and your cries are louder than their sounds,
Let your rage burn and set ablaze everything that causes your cries.

Stand mother Earth,
I stand with you,
Stand; shake these barbarians off you,
Wash them away and the impurities they have used to poison you.

Stand Mother Earth, Stand!
All they are is a disease, a war and a violence called man.

They care for you not;
they care nothing for your losses.

Stand Mother Earth, Stand!
Show them true power,
show them who you really are!

Stand Mother Earth! Stand!
Raise yourself up,
brush them off you like pests and disease.
Crush them under your feet,
For their audacious carelessness of your worth to them, and their ingratitude of what
you have given.

Stand Mother Earth! Stand!
They have never loved you, and they never will;
All they do is hurt and stab you with their machines and drills.

Stand Mother Earth! Stand!
Take back your earth and destroy the pest upon you called man.

© D M Watterson
20.09.2019

Hallows Eve

He walked up to the brown eyed girl,
Touched her gently on her arm to alert her,

"Who are you, what are you?"
His touch said.

Opening wide her mouth,
She threw back her head,
Letting him see all the souls swirling inside her;
All the souls of the dead.

Jumping back, he shouted with fear.

She looked at him and said quietly so only he would hear:
'I am hell on Earth when I die,
I am hell contained within these eyes,
I am the hell you fear,
I am the hell that will be unleashed here.

I have been made into the empress and the gate.

The wife of him,
And the mother of them.'

He gawked and stared,
Unsure of his way forward; until she said:
'I am old,
The first woman, not Eve,
I am not the one duped by the devil in the "tree",
But I am forever made to pay,
Forever judged on his mistake,
Forever blamed.

Why have I been awakened?'
He looked at her and softly said;
"It's hallows eve, the night of the dead."

Forgive me, forgive me not

Nightmare of mine,
Each night of my life.

How I paid,
I paid;
I paid;
in blood, in tears, in woe;
and in rage.

The looks I still get,
Like a gold-digging Jessabelle,
For falling in love with your ugly;
that I can't forget.

Your lies and shifting eyes tainted my energy,
Your lies stole a part of me,
Tell your ugliness to let me free.

Bound and chained to your misery,
Twisted up in your negativity,
In a maze without an escape or exit,
Just because I loved you once,
Just because I gave you a chance.

Forgive me, forgive me not,
I see you in people that you are not,
Forgive me, forgive me not,
Unbound me from this ugly heart,
Forgive me, Forgive me not,
Release me from your faults,
Forgive me, forgive me not,
I lift my heart to the skies,
Forgive me, forgive me not,
I lift my soul too,
to do what you need to do.

Forgive me, forgive me not,
Forgive me, forgive me not.

© D M Watterson
21.08.2019

Dire

Dire , is this time,
Dire is this life,
Dire, so dire,
That we must all stand together as one.

A time has been before,
Where an enemy was man,
A man who almost conquered,
Was it not for a failed plan.

Together once again we stand,
One nation,
One land,
One world,
One globe,
Against one very dangerous foe.

To the people, stay safe,
Be wise, listen and make hast,
To the people, remain calm,
Stay orderly, organized, to prevent any harm.

To the people,
At this dark hour, kneel and pray,
Speak to God,
Make amends for things done and said before it is too late.

To the people,
Take care,
Stay safe.

©DM Watterson
24.03.2020

Do not Dance the dance,

the deathly dance of the hybrid,
be a monocotyledon,
a single cell of dying.

Speak the tongue of the flowery race,
The fairy gifts within, in place,
Flit and be a wisp in the time of days,
As time runs out and all decays.

Feel the wind upon your face,
The wisdom of earth,
The voice of grace,
Listen as you cry and pray.

Hear the waves crash upon the shore,
The swelling, that swells and swells;
Towering over all,
Washing away all those intent on war.

Smell the stench of death and disease,
Rancid, fettering breathe,
Death, bloated, and rotting beneath,
Smiling with Pestilence who has been set free.

Touch the earth,
Feel its coldness and its heat,
As it shudders, cracks and breaks beneath your feet,
Know the earth has brought you to your knees.

Beg to be kind,
Beg for protection over you,
Beg only if you speak the truth,
Beg before all are fools.

© DM Watterson
18.10.2019

Crossroads

Crossroads; how cross?
Angry and stirring up an intersection of dust.
North, East, West, South,
Directions pointing to....

....another hell.

Crossroads, by the criss and the cross,
Crickety crockety,
Cross roads to hard luck.

Criss, cross, criss, cross,
Fingers behind his back,
negating the losses....
Of the criss crosses.......

Of the CRISS, CROSS, CRISS, CROSS!

Crooked plots,
Crooked losses,
Crooked, crooked, crooked , cross.

Crossroads, crooked criss, criss, crass, cross.

Waves avalanche.

As the Depths,
deeper than the ocean floor......
....strewn with bones of murdered men, and war....

....Criss, cross, a tumbling crown lost;
As its criss, cross... knocked a crown
..... off its own crooked loss....

..‾..‾..‾..‾..‾..‾

Cold

Almost apathetic,
Getting restless with apathy and its deep anesthetic,
How it stares coldly back at me,
Few emotions evoked,
Few emotions sown;
When you go inside a cold, cold soul.

To the right is the fight,
To the left is the bereaved and bereft,
The hopelessness of all that was,
and now isn't.

The deathly faith that keeps regurgitating life within,
Like a bad repeat of something eaten recent.

The cold hard lie to deny,
The cold hard truth protected from you,
From view.

If only you all knew,
No more fool,
But then nightmares and fears come true......
and then what will you do?

When seeing a sight in a temple,
masturbatory ankhs acting as phallus's'
Representative and made into disciples'
with wide smiles filling the faces of red-haired giants'
Sitting in circles;
around this witness silenced.

Naked with vision,
Naked with wisdom,
Naked with the truth concealed,
If people knew that what is isn't;
and what isn't;
is.

Cold, the truth,
Cold if you knew,
That the safest place told to you,
Is not a hell designed by lying fools,
Made of denials,

Made of the coveted knowledge of conditioning done;
Should it become known......

Cold, cold, cold,
Is a soul, that knows,
That protects those that don't,
That dismantles hand made hells breeding and living in limbo.

Cold,
Cold, cold, is its touch,
Within its warmth,
The truth of how conned,
by a symbol older than the younger,
an unveiling of truth,
a nakedness presented to you,
cold, cold, cold,
the words that present from a mouth vomited like shadows.

A Grin that stretches across an entire face;
When you realize that cold is love,
Dressed in nakedness,
Dressed in full reveal,
Dressed as is;
When we all meet our Cold Devil's within.

© DM Watterson
18.11.2019

Beloved Justice.

Lady in the night,
Queen of the darkest hour,
mother of the innocent, slain and lost.
The lady, the lady, the lady, the lady;
Never forgot.

Beloved, with bending boughs,
Hanging;
Bells of chiming time,
Ringing;
Ringing;

Ringing;

us all down....
.....
....
....
            Down.............

Into the fires of demise.

Hanging us all;
From the boughs of borrowed life.

Slitting the throats of justice,
One jugular at a time.

Tying the wrists of the law,
With blindfolded eyes.

Breaking the backs of those,
who cross her path.

Balancing the scales once more,
injustice rises before the fall.
Balancing the scales once and for all,
injustice rises before the fall

© D M Watterson
25.09.2019

Beating beaten.

Golden brown change falls from life,
As the season exits,
Another becomes a borrower of time.

Orange leaves floating down,
swaying, sashaying;
Gently,
gently all the way to the ground,
Resting there peaceful, and sound.

Dried up earth,
Dried up life,
Dried up tears,
not raining down.

Cracked and parched,
Snapping branches lacking time,
A bent old bark,
Breaking at last.

The very last leaf,
The very last seed,
The coldest night,
The saddest scene.

Shining up high,
Glistening hopefully but full of doubt,
the star of Death looking down;
beating down on life;
that has already been beaten down.

© DM Watterson
20.03.2020

A Pretty Cat

Once I saw a pretty cat,
Who had a witch that owned her back,
Fsssttt and purring whenever scratched,
By the white witch who loved her cat.

Have seen the witch of white,
The enchantress,
an oracle from another time spent;
from realms before, cursed to be undeparted?

Upon her heart engraved in bold,
The names of innocent souls,
Her blood shed for each and every;
Protecting them all from deaths plan so cleverly.

Reflecting in her eyes the wisdom of ancient many,
her soul strengthened by father time to defeat her enemies,
the White enchantress, the White High Priestess;
who through her blood shed protects the innocents death has chosen; from eternal
rest.

The White witch, High Priestess, Enchantress,
Protecting all from the Horsemen that collect.
This earthly sprite, this nymph of moonlight,
A daughter of earth, fire, water and sky.

Have you seen her pretty cat,
Who has a witch that owns her back,
Fsssttt and purring whenever scratched,
By the white witch who loves her cat?

© DM Watterson
01.08.2019

8 Years forward.

Gurgling and gasping ,
He claws her,
Gasping at her, as she stands looking at him suffocating.

It's like Total recall, she asks and almost laughs to herself;
While an image of Arnold with his eyes popping out,
And a woman with three breasts appear from her mind.

She continues to walk through this place,
Looking at bridges, roads,
Looking at skyscrapers so tall.

Looking at him now on the ground crawling.

Foaming at the mouth,
No oxygen going into his lungs,
Clawing at her,
and his own chest now.

Banging on his chest like a Tarzan,
Eyes so wide and bulbous,
He looks wild with fear.

Clawing at his throat now,
Skin and blood under his nails,
Blood and sweat streaking his throat and chest like bulging veins.

Slowing now,
Lethargic and clumsy,
Falling all over,
She watches him stop crawling and come to a halt,
As his last bit of air rattles out.

© DM Watterson
26.11.2019

A New Old Death

Death has spread its wings,
Death has surpassed,
Death is wearing a new old mask.

Color doesn't matter,
Class doesn't count,
If you are weak,
Death will find your path.

Gasping and gasping,
Falling to the ground,
This Death likes failing lungs,
and in failing hearts and bodies,
it abounds.

Gasping and Gasping,
Sweating with fever,
The Hand of death is overlooking here.

Color doesn't matter,
Class doesn't count;
If you are weak,
A new old Death will take you out of life.

© DM Watterson
30.01.2020

Ask

For Peace,
For an epiphany,
For clarity,
For your inside, to be more beautiful than your outside could ever be.

Beg;
For forgiveness,
For your sins omitted.
Beg;
For understanding,
remember the memories and lessons forgotten.

Love;
No matter what,
No matter how hard,
No matter the frustrations;
Always be filled with love, even though the journey is far.

Hope;
For humanity,
For civility,
For compassion for those things you cannot see,
For those things you cannot know indefinitely.

Have;
Faith that you are not alone,
That you will always be guided,
By the light, by the Father
By home, to the souls of the highest.

Ask;
Speak,
Be kind, undemanding,
Be humble and weak,
Show your soul, let it be seen;
Ask for help and you will receive.

© DM Watterson
13.01.2020

Be Compelled

If you wish upon a star,
Makes no difference who you are,
When you wish upon a star,
Your dreams come true.

No, they don't!
That isn't how it is,
You work, you do a gig,
You do whatever it takes to get it done;
Free life that's a load of bullshit!

No such thing as a free gig,
Watch the skies,
The stars are falling too quick,
One, two, three, four;
Five, six, and seven is knocking on our door!

You laughed too quick,
Moved too slick,
Thought you were smarter;
But nothing outsmarts the smartness Bitches!

Seven Stars and seven trumpets,
About to get nasty,
For all you dumb f@ckers!

Reveal, revel, reveal, revel,
Its time up assholes!
Be Compelled!

Before I start,

Before I begin;
How I have waited to tell you everything!

"What? Why? Me? I?"

I have known your pain,
I have known your betrayals,
I have seen your heartache,
And I have seen the clogging of your veins.

Before I start,
Before I begin;
Before it is the end of the beginning of everything!

"Where? When? You? This whole time?"

I have seen your tears,
I have seen your fears,
Take my hand,
I will show you years.

Together at all times,
Heaven has been found,
This way,
You will be just fine.

Go towards the field and the tree,
Right there is eternal family.

Blackened skies

Raining down from above,
Blackened skies filled with hateful guns,
Missiles pummel the ground,
The sky blackened out.

The Ground breaking,
cracking and shaking,
foundations fissured,
buildings broken holding survivors prisoner.

© **DM Watterson**
17.01.2020

Asunder

Twas an eve before last,
I had my hand upon my heart,
Solemnly promising allegiance,
Swearing to be protector and leader.

I weep now for this place,
That is so filled with hate,
A place I called home,
Now rent apart by those.

All that has been built,
Has been torn asunder,
Destroyed,
Demoted to a place of foe,
a broken place of broken souls.

© DM Watterson
17.01.2020

Watching you, judging you

You do something unforgettable,
People doubt,
You're just not capable,
Every time you fail,
Mocked, laughed at;

"Not that smart are you now"
"NOT SUCH A HOT SHOT NOW HEY!"
"But you're so smart, smarter than that"
"Maybe you're an idiot savant!"
"Maybe you should just, keep quiet"
"hahahaha hahaha, haha haha"

Watching you, judging you,
Waiting for you to fall,
Watching you, judging you,
Waiting for you to scream at them all,
Watching you, judging you,

Yes, I did it, yea I did,
Call me an idiot,
Ask for forgiveness for it,
Yes, I did it, yea I did,
Call me a retard,
Call me slow again.

Coz now I am watching you,
Now I am judging you,
Watching you, judging you,
Watching you, judging you,

Death

The sound of Scythe,
Raking up bones on the ground,
Death collects them all,
Death is collecting the world,
An old debt owed to death.

Walking in his cloak,
With his scythe;
his skeletal hand in sight.

© DM Watterson

Fillet Knife

Tied to the table,
Wrists locked in metal clasps,
Wriggling, yanking,
Wrists now oiled with blood.

Walking up to the table,
Lifting a fillet knife,
Slowly filleting the fleshy side.

Screams and wails and then the silence of passed out;
Moaning again while coming around.

Still tied to the table,
Still bleeding to the floor,
Still chained to enable,
Still chained to ignored.

Blood soaked apron in sight,
Heavy gloved hands,
Holding a bloody fillet knife.

A fluorescing light flickers,
Then goes out,
Pitch darkness;
Filling with screams from a fillet knife.

© DM Watterson
31.10.2019

Forgive me

I cannot stop these people,
I cannot change their minds,
I cannot show them what I have seen,
On the panoramic lens in my mind's eye.

Forgive me,
I have failed,
Forgive me for your raping,
Forgive me for all the abuse,
Forgive me,
I have failed you.

I cannot stop them,
I cannot stop them killing.
I cannot stop them drilling,
I cannot stop anything.

Forgive me,
Forgive me I am a loss and a fool;
Forgive me for being.

Forgive me,
I am lost inside the dark, selfish, cruel, and evil.

But, not Human being,
The worst kind,
of kind,
to be.

Forgive me,
Forgive me.

Helpless in knowing

A Cloud of Sadness,
As a cloak surrounds me;
made of calmness.

A hand in mine,
"you did all you could child";
Softly spoken into my mind's eye.

I bow my head;
Sighing and frowning,
biting my bottom lip;
To stop myself from crying.

Hand on my shoulder now,
Gently squeezing,
To comfort my mind.

I sit still and inert ,
Quietly paging through all the images shown;
Asking what I must do,
feeling helpless in knowing.

© DM Watterson
06.02.2020

Higher

The wicked will not know,
The wicked will not understand,
The wicked cannot see,
The wicked carry on petty;
The wicked carry on like all is going to plan.

Guard yourselves against the darkness,
Living In so many hearts,
It has already taken a home here,
Found residence in the darkest parts.

Tit, for tat,
Two wrongs, make it right, don't they?
DON'T THEY?
Tit for TAT,
the combat of a wasted man!

Bigger, better, higher,
Strive for the highest,
Exalt for he is coming!
Exalt for the savior is among us!

Higher, higher,
Strive to be higher,
Love and kindness,
IS the only antidote,
to evil and blindness!

© **DM Watterson**
23.03.2020

Love,

Love is patient,
Love never dies,
Love doesn't push, shove or hit;
Love never gives you black eyes.

Love is sometimes firm to be kind,
Love can be tough when there is a fight,
Love ,
real love;
never runs away when it gets too hard,
nor does it turn its back on you;
when you need it on your side.

Love will go through all,
Love will give you a choice,
Love is the proverbial horse,
Armored, muscled, strong, fast and loyal.

Love will wait, and wait endlessly,
Love will swallow its tears,
Love will come out of the dark,
When love knows you fear.

Love will carry every burden,
Love will carry every load,
Love will never leave you alone,
Love should be the heart of every Loving home.

©DM Watterson

Marked with murder,

Marked with pain,
Marked with death;
War in wait.

Faster, faster,
Speed of light,
Eyes upon ,
Red eyed satellite,
Blinking blue,
Blinking red…

Counting down;
Days till death.

Prayers made,
Dark magic played,
From one aide to another's aid,
Darkness paid.

Hands together,
Words of grace;
For Protection sought,
The cost paid.

Counting down;
To the day.

Marked with murder,
Marked with Pain,
Marked with death;
War in wait.

© DM WATTERSON
30.10.2019

Natures rage

As the flames hiss,
crackle and lick at terra's face,
Sucking life from everything,
Cremating homes,
Turning man made heaviness into ashes;
and forgotten bones.

"Should have listened,
Should have listened!"
Mother natures pissed roaring in your ears!

Heat ablaze,
Burning flesh from a trapped 'soul's face,
Screaming out in pain,
A casualty of many to come from the flames.

"Should have listened!
Should have Listened!

While the heat burns all away,
While the haze upon the horizon seen,
Can never be erased,
Forever aflame,
Forever blackened;
By natures rage.

A Friend of Death

Of all the souls,
Of all the chosen,
Of all the knowledge betrothed,
Of all the knowledge birthed down from the old ones.

As I speak, I pray,
As my hands clasp ,
My knees drop to the ground as I say;

"those I touch,
Those who seek,
Those I have loved,
And for those I have wept,
Your souls are safe and kept.

Your souls have been traded;
They have been bought back from death."

Of all the souls,
Of all those traded,
Of all those taken, harmed and degraded.

As I Speak, as I pray,
As my hands clasp,
My knees drop to the ground as I say:

"those I touch,
Those who seek,
Those I have loved,
And for those I have wept,
Your souls are safe and kept.

Your souls have been traded;
They have been bought back from death."

© DM Watterson
05.11.2019

The House of Dark

Every night I wonder there;
To a place of dark horrors,
Secrets, and plots;
A place that was not always dark.

I walk in the gardens,
Greeting the old dead,
Canines, cats,
family and friends.

Painted in black magic,
On every brick,
Old black magic;
Smeared in dark blood that is thick.

Masses of food, meat, and sweet things.
Hidden treasures;
Stolen things within.

I will not go inside;
On the outstand I stand,
Watching all those waiting;
For justice and death to play their hands.

Scores of souls await a death,
Scores of souls waiting for justice to collect.

The House of dark,
Protected by him,
Mistaken for God;
Trusted as friend.

The House of Dark,
Not a House of God.
The House of Dark;
coming to an end.
The House of Dark;
Where an old devil lives.

© DM Watterson
21.01.2020

The Russian Plot.

You are looking at me,
Staring at me,
Just like your unknown enemy;
In a car, moving.

Together;
Side by side,
You, and a dark-haired man;
With darkness plotting in his mind.

A plot underfoot,
An assassination,
A planned bullet;
An end to a presidents placement.

He plays the game of the lesser,
To assure you;
That he is not a danger;
But his true mind to you,
Is a stranger.

A friend of yours,
An ally, named China,
Will help you find this dark man,
With his dark mind planning to harm you.

A Russian plot,
Unfolding quick, and hot.
A Russian Plot,
One of your own is going to try take your spot,
By placing a bullet through your head and your heart.

© DM Watterson
09.01.2020

We prepare for War

As eves arise and fall ,
As moons descend to the hellish floor,
As dawn creeps upon the heavens ,
Streaking the clouds with Arrows and swords,
Signals to the earths devils.

We prepare for War.

Rising up like a mouth of rancid vomit,
Bitter, sour taste of dishonest,
The scalding burn catching a throat,
Screaming ....GO!

A warning from the Hallows,
A caution to the challengers,
A light to those that seek the truth.

As the eve arises and the moon falls,
As the old day dies, and the new day dawns,
We prepare for War.

© DM Watterson
28.10.2019

Unworthy

Tempted, daily;
Praying fervently for you to save me.
From these thoughts, from these desires,
from my flesh constantly setting itself on fire.
Tempted daily;
By envy, by need of simple everyday things,
by plenty;
Praying fervently for you to save me.
Tempted; constantly-
To give in, to let go,
to let myself just be and wish,
to have the things of this world,
just as it were a fruit filled dish.
Tempted, Tempted,
to the point of tormented,
that I have become such a boring soul.
Almost dull with trying to be pure,
dull trying to be more, dull,
so dull I am near invisible.
Tempted, so Tempted,
I dare not pick up a pen,
I dare not sketch,
I dare not listen to a song,
or even read a book,
in case that is all it will take,
for me to be back where I started,
back looking.
Tempted, so damn tempted;
I feel myself filling with despair,
with ordinariness,
with lackluster to spare.
Praying daily;
praying for you to save me,
as I am so unworthy of your mercy and your grace.
So unworthy,
so damn unworthy;
I feel lost within this place.

22.06.2022

My weapon; my pen.

It's just like before;
Like all of them, all four.
Light filled eyes, that fade at first,
and slowly the light dies until nothing looks back,
but the reflections of hurt.

The light dies in their eyes,
and they look like the dead,
except they don't know it yet.
I always know before they do;
that's it's over, that it's through.

I keep hoping I will feel fulfilled;
like some of that light will spill inside me still.
Empty and hollow is how it is;
Except when HE smiles inside of me.

Hoping and praying for the rage to dissipate,
for the pain and the sorrow of years to be gone,
or to abate.

Hoping that something,
someone can feel it too;
Feel the emptiness that is constantly filling,
constantly overthrowing,
a game of who will win it,
throat tied by a noose,
strangling all hope into doom.

Hoping that the heartache will wash away;
That the disappointment will find a grave,
and whatever hope I have left,
will lead the way.

Hoping that my prayers will appear,
that humanity will all of a sudden see;
will suddenly hear.
Hoping that the few I have let in;
will comprehend the pain of a lonely soul wasted and spent.

Hoping that those like me;
who fought Him;
will finally believe,

will repent, and finally see.

Hoping that just one word,
one sentence I type or pen;
will etch itself in, to bring joy and faith again.

A lonely soul I am,
no matter how many I see,
no matter how many I hear,
no matter how many tears,
no matter how many screams;
I have witnessed and seen.

My sword, my pen, it is no gun;
With tortured eyes that barely hide years of neglect and abuse,
my pen is my sword; the weapon I use.

I will swing my sword;
ink pouring into puddles that form sentences and soul wrenching words;
I will swing my sword;
tearing out dead hearts to make them find a way to beat,
a weird Shelley's Frankenstein,
but for Him.

I will swing with every bit of rage that will not leave;
with every bit of sorrow that has made a home inside me;
with every bit of heartache that beats my broken heart;
with every bit of degradation that has torn this soul apart.

My weapon, my pen;
much bigger than the voice I have been given.
My weapon, my pen;
guided by Him.

Made in the USA
Columbia, SC
20 July 2022